APONI

The White Witch Of Salem

To my amazing friends and family who encouraged me to write this book. A special thank you to Jonah Casner and Thomas Fisk who helped with the research for this book.

Then to my cover artist "Santhar"did a fantastic job.

Table of Contents

Where It began

Hello my name is Aponi and I am going to tell you what really happened during the Salem witch trials. I was hidden from the town because when I was born, I was born with pale skin, red hair and green eyes. My father was from the Naumkeag tribe and my mother was one of the survivors from the war between the two.

The townsfolk believe that red hair is stolen from the flames of hell by the bearer and green eyes are a clear sign of being a witch and evil but what I have seen in the last year show that the only evil to conspire here was from greed and fear of the townsfolk themselves. They think that if you look differently or believe differently you work for the so-called black man that everyone fears but one of their own was working for the devil. I know true evil when I see it and it was hiding in plain sight and right under their noses. This is what really happened in Salem.

Everything started with one foggy night. I was walking through the woods on my way to my cottage when someone was talking to the black man; Something seemed off about him.

"What is your plan master?" a man asked.

"You will know when it happens. This town will bend to chaos and panic when I am done with it," the black man explained.

"Very well master," the man replied.

"Do as I say and you will have unimaged power," the black man said, "but if you fail me you will be punished,"

"Yes master," the man responded, watching as, man vanished in the fog.

I hid behind a tree and some bushes. There was no way what was coming would be good. Once both men were gone I came out from behind the tree and went to my house. It was clear that my magic was not the only magic in Salem, but this magic has a dark overhanging sense of black magic to it.

The next morning I went into town and it was oddly quiet. A group of young girls were talking to William Stoughon. It was unclear what they were saying, I don't think it was good but I know better to get too close to the people in this town. Bridget Bishop was accused of being a witch because two of her husbands died and she is known to be a bit rebellious. I met her and I know how they died of natural causes.

A few days later I heard strange noises outside not far from my cottage. I crept through the woods to see the girls dancing in the woods and chanting. In the tree line stood a dark figure. The girls slowly got louder and louder. Out of all of them I could only clearly make out two of the girls. The first one was nine year old Elizabeth Parris who was known as Betty. The second one was eleven year old Abigail Williams, Betty's cousin.

"Come to us master," the girls chanted, and slowly spinning in circles holding hands, "hear our cries and walk this land. It is time for these people to obey us. Make them fear your power. We call to you our almighty master. Come to us and walk through this land."

"It is time for me to leave, girls, someone is coming. Keep chanting and dancing. You will enjoy what comes next," the black man said, as he vanished in the fog.

"Yes sir," they replied.

I could not believe what I had just seen and heard. There is no doubt in mind that the supposed black man was only here to cause trouble. I don't know who this man really is but I will find out.

Crack! A stick broke behind me as the girls were dragged away from the woods. As I turned around he was standing there staring at me.

"My, my what do we have here?" he asked, "a spy?"

"Leave me alone,"

"Now why would I do that young lady?" he smirked, stroking my hair, "such pretty red hair. I have seen you in the town and in the woods. Why do you hide your red hair?"

I smacked his hand away, "leave me alone. I know nothing good can come from someone as evil as you! Someone with as much power as you should not pray on, children or foolish men, but instead you choose to use them to gain more power!"

"So we have a brave little white witch. Your better bet is to stay out of this," the man warned as he left me standing there, fearing for my life.

I could not help but fear this man. The darkness around him makes me wonder who he truly is.

A few days had passed and the girls began to suffer from so-called fits. Elizabeth Parris and Abigail Williams were the first to succumb to these fits. They would roll around on the floors, bark like a dog and scream uncontrollably. By the time their families called the doctor it was January 20th of 1692.

"Doctor, may I have a word with you?" the black man asked.

"Yes, of course sir. How can I be of service to you?" William Griggs replied.

William Griggs is the town's reproach of a doctor.

"I thought it would be best to tell you that there are a few witches running around our tiny little town of Salem. It is possible that one might have bewitched the girls at the Parris house," the black man asked..

"Oh my, thank you for the warning, good sir," William Griggs replied with fear in his face.

"You are welcome doctor," the black man responded, walking away with a sly smirk.

William Griggs arrived at the house while the two girls were in the middle of a screaming fit. He waited for them to stop screaming to speak with Reverend Samuel Parris.

"When did this all start?" William Griggs asked.

"A few days ago. It has only worsened. I don't know what could be wrong with them," Reverend Samuel Parris explained.

"I can only think of one thing this could be," William Griggs said, "I was told there are few witches in town."

"What are you getting at, doctor?" Reverend Samuel Parris asked, startled.

"I strongly believe that your girls have been bewitched," William Griggs answered.

"Are you sure that this is what is wrong with them?" Reverend Samuel Parris asked, shocked by the answer.

"Yes I am certain that they have been bewitched," William Griggs replied.

"Then I will call a witch hunter to town," Reverend Samuel Parris said, "you need to let Chief Justice William Stoughon know and have him let the others know."

Witch Hunt

As I walked past the reverend's house I saw a man, new in Salem, dressed in dark clothes and was tall. I believe he is a witch hunter.

"So how do you think we are going to find the witches?" Reverend Samuel Parris asked.

"I need your servant to prepare what is called witch cakes. I will need some urine from one of the girls, rye meal, ashes and baked. As for the urine I will need it from your daughter," the hunter said.

"Is that all? Who will eat the cakes?" Reverend Samuel Parris asked.

"I will feed the cakes to the dog. From there, the dog that eats it will tell us who the witch is, in this house," the hunter finished. "How many do you think are here?" Reverend Samuel Parris asked.

"It is hard to say," the hunter said, walking to his horse.

I choose to follow this man. It did not take much to figure out that he was working for someone more powerful, someone just like the man I saw a few weeks ago with the girls. The reproached poor excuse of a witch hunter met up with the black man, encouraging my suspicion

"I saw a red head in town. She is pale and has green eyes. That young lady would make an easier target to frame as a witch; she will stick out like a sore thumb," the hunter pointed out.

"Leave that one be," the black man said, "for I have plans for her."

"Are you foolish, master? This is the easiest target in Salem. Those girls will not help you as much as you want," the hunter remarked.

"Do not question your master! If you go after that young lady I will see to it you pay for it," the black man warned, "the girls will say who bewitched them and from there you help cause chaos. Disobey me and I will punish you severely for it. This is the only time I will tell you."

"Yes master," the hunter said, briskly walked away

"Why are you here?"

"Well, well, well looks like I have myself a little spy," the black man said.

"Leave this town be,"

"Now why would I do that little witch?" he asked, walking closer, "this town doesn't care for you. So why do you care about what happens to it?"

"They may not care for me but innocent people will be killed by this chaos,"

"How is that my problem?" the black man asked.

"Because all life is to be treasured and protected. To kill someone because you enjoy the thrill of it is wrong, immoral and evil."

"But I am not the one killing them. They will do that all on their own. You will see after the board is set I will not have to lift a finger," the black man smirked.

"It doesn't matter you still started it,"

"You can't stop me, little one. I feed off fear and Salem is rich in fear and hatred," he smirked once more.

"Unless they find out you are here. Then they will hunt you, not their own. I know you are not human. I may not be as strong as you or as smart as you but I know people's fear can change. I will figure out how to stop you."

"You are a foolish little white witch. You have a chance for power and you are choosing these pathetic people over it," the black man said, as he vanished in the fog.

I snuck my way back to the Reverend's house and watched through the window.

"Give the cake to the dog. Once it has eaten the cake it will find the witch as long as they are in the house," the hunter said.

"Ok," Reverend Samuel Parris replied, feeding the cake to the dog.

I can't believe Reverend Samuel Parris is buying the fools act. This is clearly fake but he is so blinded by fear he can't see past it.

"The witch is not in the house right now," the hunter said, gathering his things, "the girls should be able to see the specter of who is bewitching them."

"Should we ask them the next time a fit starts?" Reverend Samuel Parris asked.

"Yes," the hunter answered and left.

It did not take long for the girls to have another fit. This started the trials.

"Tituba, Sarah Good and Sarah Osborne are the ones attacking us!" Elizabeth Parris screamed.

"Tituba was talking to the devil," Abigail Williams sobbed, covering her face.

"I will have them arrested and we will hold a trial," Chief Justice William Stoughon said.

Trials

"Sarah Good, are you a witch?" Chief Justice William Stoughon asked, "if you plead guilty and give up your other witches we will let you live. If you plead innocent and found guilty you will be hanged."

"I am no witch your honor," Sarah Good answered.

"These girls say you are," Chief Justice William Stoughon replied.

"Maybe they are mistaken, but I am no witch," Sarah Good said.

"I am not mistaken! She is a witch!" Abigail Williams yelled.

"I am in church every Sunday! I come early and stay late! I am no witch! This is the children's way to get attention! They have acted out and are looking for someone to place blame upon. They have no proof of these wildish claims!" Sarah Good yelled, standing up.

"I think we have heard enough from Sarah Good. We can move to the next woman," William Fiske said.

William Fiske was a member of the jury.

"Every well Sarah Osborne, take the stand," Chief Justice William Stoughon said, waving her over, "are you a witch?"

"I am no witch," Sarah Osborne answered calmly.

"It is the same deal with you that I made Sarah Good," Chief Justice William Stoughon replied, "if you plead guilty and give up your other witches you will live. If you are found guilty and plead innocent you will be hanged. Now I will ask again, are you a witch?"

"No, I am not a witch. Now are we done with this nonsense?" Sarah Osborne said, looking him in the eyes.

"Have you ever spoken to the devil?" Chief Justice William Stoughon asked.

"No I never spoke to the devil," Sarah Osborne replied calmly.

"Fine it is late. We are done for today. We start first thing in the morning with Tituba. Put these women in jail for tonight," Chief Justice William Stoughon said, walking out.

I choose to follow him. He waited outside the courthouse for the rest of the townspeople to leave before he walked into the woods. He was around where the girls were dancing around like fools.

It left me to wonder if Chief Justice William Stoughon was working with the black man that had sent the town into a hysteria. Was he to blame for this whole ordeal? Maybe he is a pawn for the black man.

"What do you want Stoughon?" the black man asked, "this had better be good,"

"The women the girls had picked out are claiming innocence. If Tituba doesn't plead guilty your plans will not work," William Stoughon said. "How will I get her to talk?"

"She will talk because she wants to live and will not take the chance on being found guilty," the black man smirked, "just wait this will see."

"Yes master," William Stoughon said, leaving to go home.

"So you are indeed the devil himself,"

"I didn't even hear this time. Yes I am the devil," he said walking closer, "still hiding your hair I see."

"Leave these people be. They are not witches. No one in this town has done anything wrong. You are the only guilty party here!"

"What about my pawns? This would not have been possible without them," he remarked.

"Like you said, they are your pawns. They are doing your bedding out of fear or desire."

"They have the option to say no," he replied.

"Do they really?"

"You think I am lying about this," he said.

"I know who you are. You can't fool me.

If they have hope you lose control over them,"

"If you do anything to save this town you will regret it!" he yelled.

"I see you don't like people challenging you. Well I will save this town from your grip and no matter what I will not regret it."

"You are a fool, but you do not have the power to beat me," he chuckled, and left.

The next morning they started to question Tituba.

"Have you spoken to the devil?" Chief Justice William Stoughon asked.

"Yes I have," Tituba answered.

"What did he tell you to do?" Chief Justice William Stoughon asked.

"To harm the young girls in Salem," Tituba said.

"Tell us how this happened," Captain Thomas Fiske ordered.

"I followed a great black dog until I saw a black man in the woods outside the Parris's household. The devil came to me and asked that I do his bidding. I signed his devil's book using my blood. At his feet was a black rat, a hog and a red rat. In the tree branch above him sat a small yellow bird. Standing behind him stood four women and one man," Tituba weaved her web of lies.

There is no doubt that someone put her up to this. There are a few possibilities of who could have.

"Can you tell me who they were?" Chief Justice William Stoughon asked.

"I was only able to tell who two of the women were. They are Sarah Good and Sarah Osborne," Tituba said, pointing at them.

"Lock them up and get these women out of my sights now!" Chief Justice William Stoughon yelled, slamming his gable down dismissing the court.

"She is lying! We are not witches!" Sarah Good and Sarah Osborne screamed, trying to fight back.

Greed Or Fear

As matters worsened greed and fear filled the town. Neighbors turned on each other to gain more land.

"Rebecca Nurse murdered my babies using supernatural forces. My daughter Ruth said that Rebecca's spirit tried to tempt her iniquity," Goody Putnam sobed with tears rolling down her cheeks.

"Have Rebecca Nurse locked up to await her trial," Chief Justice William Stoughon said, looking at John Dane.

"Sir, she is at church all the time. Rebecca Nurse would not harm a child you know this.

She is 71 years old. What use would she have to talk to the devil?" John Dane pleaded.

"The girls say she is a witch and Goody Putnam's babies have died with no natural explanation she is to be tried," Chief Justice William Stoughon said.

It was not hard to hear what anyone in this town said. They all talked so loud.

I knew it was all an act. The Putnams were bitter enemies with the Nurses. Why no one took this under consideration when Goody Putnam accused Rebecca Nurse of being a witch. Rebecca was a God fearing person unlike the first three victims. She and her husband owned a 300 acre farm. Poor Rebecca Nurse was being put on trial because of greed.

"Are you a witch?" Captain Thomas Fiske asked.

"No I am not a witch," Rebecca Nurse replied.

"Have you harmed the girls?" Captain Thomas Fiske asked.

"No, I have not harmed the girls and I am no witch! God knows I am innocent," Rebecca Nurse yelled.

"Have you spoken to the black man?" Captain Thomas Fiske questioned.

"No I have not." Rebecca Nurse said.

"Are you a witch?" Chief Justice William Stoughon asked.

"I can say before my Eternal Father I am innocent and God will clear my innocence! The Lord knows I have not hurt them! I am an innocent person!" Rebecca Nurse yelled.

The trial went on for most of the day. They asked her the same questions over and over. I knew I had to try to help her so I left some of the church members a petition to save her. About 39 people signed it and risked their lives to save her.

"Rebecca Nurse was found not guilty," Chief Justice William Stoughon said.

It was clear he was not pleased by the results of the trial. This is when they brought in Goody Hobbs.

"But she is one of us!" Rebbeca Nurse yelled.

Anyone could tell she was overwhelmed but Chief Justice William Stoughon and Captain Thomas Fiske did not care one bit.

"What do you mean by that?" Captain Thomas Fiske asked, turning to Rebbeca Nurse.

When she did not answer them the verdict changed to guilty. She was unable to hear them ask the question so she couldn't have answered them. Chief Justice William Stoughon had her sent straight to the jail where they were holding the others.

Outside of the courthouse stood the black man under a tree with a smirk on his face. I would have loved to knock it right off of his face.

On my way he began to follow me.

"It is amazing how quick they turn on each other," the black man said.

"She was no witch."

"They believe differently. You tried to save the poor sweet old woman and failed," he smirked, "you see fear will always be stronger than hope. You can't win, little witch."

"It still wouldn't stop me from trying to save Salem from the lights of you."

"You will fail. Greed and fear are stronger," he said.

"We will see about that."

"That is what roanoke thought but they were wrong," the black man said and walked away.

First victims

The day Bridget Bishop's third husband died the town of Salem accused her of being a witch for the second time. She was always a bit rebellious, so that did not help her case either.

I don't know how to help her. There is no way that anyone would help her like they did with Rebecca Nurse. Not many people liked her.

"I am innocent I say," Bridget Bishop said.

"Speak the truth, are you a witch!" William Stoughon yelled.

"No, I am not a witch! I did not make a pact with the devil," Bridget screamed.

"So you are saying that these girls are lying. They saw you spectral," William Stoughon asked, "you have had three husbands and all three have died."

"I said I am not a witch! I did not murder ay of my husbands," Bridget yelled.

"Did you bewitch them?" William asked, "did you make a pact with the devil?"

"I did not bewitch them. I did not make a pact with the devil and I have already said I am not a witch! Why will you not listen to me?" Bridget yelled.

"She is a witch! We saw her spirit talking to the black man!" the girls screamed. "They are lying, I am not a witch!" Bridget Bishop yelled.

"Owww! Her specter is stabbing me! Make her stop!"Ann Putnam screamed and dropped to the floor.

"She is faking it! I am doing no such thing!" Bridget Bishop yelled.

"Make her stop! Oww! She is attacking!" Ann Putnam screamed. "Bridget Bishop, I will ask one last time. Are you a witch?" Captain Thomas Fiske yelled.

"I am not a witch! How many times must I tell you! These girls are lying to you people!" Bridget Bishop yelled.

"Bridget Bishop, you have been found guilty of witchcraft," Captain Thomas Fiske said.

Bridget Bishop was hanged a few days later. Sheriff George Coriwn had her hanged on June,10 1692.

A month later they had Rebecca Nurse hanged.

"I told you there is no way to save this town. Now a few are already dead. Salem has no hope," the black man said, from behind me.

"I will save Salem. There is always hope."

"We will see how far hope goes when most of Salem is dead," he smirked, "I am just getting started."

The next day the reproach witch hunter came back. Someone claimed that witches had bewitched a few dogs. They also said a witches cat was running amuck. He killed both dogs then said they were innocent because they did not come back to life. As for the cat they spent days looking for the black cat and did not find it.

"Excuse me miss, I have noticed you around town but you don't talk to anyone. Why is that?" the hunter asked, following me though the woods.

"What do you want?"

"What makes you ask that?" he asked.

"I know who you work for. I have seen you talking to him. It would be a shame if they found out the reproach of a witch hunter they hired is working for the devil."

"You wouldn't dare," he said, grabbing my arm.

"I would. You and your master have cost innocent people to die. You are nothing more than another one of his pawns. I bet you will be easier to expose than the others in Salem."

"If you are not careful I will see you on the stands," the hunter warned.

"I do not fear a fool like you,"

"You should fear me little lady," he said, leaning in closer.

"Why should I? I don't fear your all mighty master and you have no power,"

"You soon will," he smirked and walked away.

After he walked deeper into the woods he stopped.

"Master, what are you doing here?" the hunter asked.

I creeped a bit closer hiding in a bush hoping to find out why they were really here.

"I told you to stay away from the young witch!" the black man yelled.

"Master, she is no threat to our plans. Why do you want me to leave her be? She is the easiest target in Salem," he foolishly asked.

"She may seem like the easiest target in Salem but don't be fooled! She comes from a long line of witches! One slip up and my plans will be ruined!" the black man yelled, raising his hand.

"All the more reason to rid the town of her," the hunter said.

"I said no!" the black man yelled, grabbing him by his throat, "if you question my orders again you will pay the price. Do you understand?"

"Yes, master," the hunter said, clawing at the black man's hand.

"Good now go find the girls. I have a few more targets for them," the black man said, letting go of the hunter's neck.

"Who are they?" the hunter asked, standing back up.

"Philip and Mary English will do for now," the black man said, vanishing into the fog.

I rushed to the English house and left them a note warning them that they were the next people who would be accused of being witches and should find someone who could help them.

Luckily they received the note because the hunter had already reached the girls.

"Philp, look , someone left us a note," Mary said, handing it to him.

"Let's hope this person is wrong but just in case I will set some money aside. We might need it," Philip said, looking at the note.

"Why?" Mary asked, walking closer to him.

"Because one of the girls, are going to accuse us of being witches," Philip said.

"Looks like we have a guardian angel looking out for Salem," Mary replied.

Someone tried to have Spectral evidence removed from the court because it was unfair and only the girls who claimed to be bewitched could use it. Unfortunately the request was denied. So now the person being accused had to hope that the jury was on their side, but the girls made that hard for their target.

Ann Putnam and Mary Walcott even put four year old Dorothy Good in jail for witchcraft. Under pressure little Dorothy confessed to being a witch in hopes of seeing her mother. That was on March 24, 1692.

Times Up

I was on my way home and a stick broke behind me.

"Well so far you have helped five people escape being hanged for witchcraft. It doesn't matter though. They are still hanging people and the more people they kill the closer I get to their souls. Willing to give up now?" the black man smirked.

"That is what this is about? Their souls but why?"

"You were right before. I am the devil and the more souls I have the stronger I get. This is why you will not win. Your so-called hope can't fix what they have done here and it is too late for you to save them," he said, walking closer, "you could join me and have more power then you could imagine young witch."

"Go back to hell I will never help a self centered fool. Life is to be protected not taken,"

"It will be wise to stay out of my way from now on then," he warned.

"In your dreams,"

After that I began sneaking food to the jail for his victims. I made sure to only go at night so it was harder for anyone to see me and never giving any of them my name. The less people that die the less of a hold he will have on Salem.

Giles Corey refused to stand trial so they pressed him to death. He was an 81 year old man who had spoken out at his wife's trial.

John Proctor was one of them on trial because he spoke out against the trials. He said that the girls were liars and had no clue how right he was. He was found guilty.

"You see there is no way to save mankind. Trust me I have been watching them for thousands of years. They only get worse with time," the black man said, from under the tree where they just hung five people.

"You have not won yet."

"Oh, but I have, little witch," he smirked.

"No you have not yet and Giles Corey is proof and John Proctor is proof that not everyone is fooled by your pawns."

"True but one is dead and the other is waiting to be hanged, right?" he asked.

"How long do you think that they will fall for this?"

"That doesn't matter," he said, looking at me confused.

"You will not win"

"You are better off to join me," he said leaving.

A few days later they hanged John Proctor, Reverend George Burroughs and Martha Carrier along with a few others. They said Martha Carrier aspired to be the queen of hell. All of them were innocent. Reverend George Burroughs even said a prayer and spoke scripture from the bible. The crowd tried to stop the hanging but they were told even the devil lies and pretends to be an angel.

Salem's only hope was to uproot the evil and expose them or force their hands. This means I need to take a chance.

"Chief Justice William Stoughon may I have a word?"

"Yes you may," he answered.

"Good because it is time we talk,"

"What is this about, young lady?" he asked, considered.

"I know who you are working for. That those girls are lying through their teeth and that the witch hunter is helping cause this panic. So this is where you end this fake witch hunt or you might be the next target. I will tell everyone that you are the one who is really working for the black man."

"Oh really? What makes you think you are safe from me and the others then?" he smirked.

"You saw the witch hunter's neck right? Your boss did that because he was thinking the same thing you are right now. So go ahead, try it."

"He would not do that to me," he laughed.

"You are nothing more than his pawn. You can't even see that can you? He wants your soul and the more people you are at fault for killing the closer he gets to keeping it. But I have only been watching all of you closely. What would I know?"

"Who are you?" he asked.

"I am no fool you will not get my name. Think carefully about your next move. Oh and to be sure this town's witch hunt ends I went higher up in the food chain. This will stop."

I could tell he was rattled by that visit. Sadly the visit didn't help much. Martha Cory and seven others were hanged on September 22.

"I told you there is no saving them," the black man said from my doorway.

"There is a way,"

"I know you threatened Chief Justice William Stoughon a few days ago too. I thought I told you to stay out of my way," he said stepping inside.

"True you did but the truth is I don't care. Salem is my town and I will protect it from the lights of you. I asked you to leave so now

I will scare your pawns into telling the truth or calling the witch hunt off,"

"You are foolish, you could have all the power in the world but you throw the chance away for mortals. Who could care less," he smirked.

"Power is not everything and it is not worth the loss of innocent lives."

"Power is worth any cost. If you wish to be strong you must be willing to take lives to gain power," he smirked.

"No, someone's strength is not measured by their power but their courage and wisdom. Your rain over this town ends now."

After they hung those eight I wrote a letter to Governor Sir William Philips saying that they were going to accuse his wife of witchcraft. It might have been a lie but he shut down the witch trials for good in Salem.

"Chief Justice William Stoughon,"

"You again my master is displeased with you, white witch." Chief Justice William Stoughon said.

"Is he displeased with me or you?"

"How do you know that? He asked, startled.

"Governor Sir William Philips shutdown the witch trials. Your master gets no more souls because of it. I do know one more thing. For you to get to this place of power you made a deal with him and sold your soul to the black man."

"How do you know this?" he asked, puzzled.

"I don't think that matters. Does it? The real question is do you want it back?"

"Of course I do! What kind of a question is that?" he yelled.

"You need to right your wrongs to start. That means you need to admit you were wrong to Salem and tell them what really happened here. He doesn't have the girls' souls but he has your's and the witch hunter's."

"I will not! They killed each other! All I did was keep order!" he yelled, "I did nothing wrong!"

"So be it. Believe that if you wish. I was going to help you but now you are on your own."

"You can't help me, you work for him!" Chief Justice William Stoughon yelled.

"A white witch does not serve the devil. We serve nature and protect all life. I could have helped you but you are willing to take no blame for what was partially your fault. One day the truth will come out and you will regret it."

"None of this will come out. As we speak I am having Captain Thomas Fiske, William Fiske and John Dane burn the court records," he smirked.

"It is hard to believe how foolish some of you can be. Even if you burn the proof here this still happened. You can't erase what you and the rest of Salem has done in this last year no matter how hard you try. The story of Salem will be passed down from one generation to the next. Your master may have lost but you still gave up your soul."

As I walked away the Black man was standing in the tree line over the dead witch hunter. He may have lost this battle but the war is far from over.